A TEMPLAR BOOK

Produced by The Templar Company plc,
Pippbrook Mill, London Road, Dorking, Surrey RH4 1JE, Great Britain.

Text copyright © *The Land of Blue Mountains* 1926-1953 by Darrell Waters Limited
Illustration and design copyright © 1993 by The Templar Company plc
Enid Blyton is a registered trademark of Darrell Waters Limited

This edition produced for Parragon Books,
Unit A, Central Trading Estate, Bath Road, Brislington, Bristol.

This book contains material first published as
The Land of Blue Mountains in Enid Blyton's Sunny Stories
and Sunny Stories between 1926 and 1953.

Illustrated by Maggie Downer

Printed and bound in Italy

ISBN 1 85813 377 7

Enid Blyton's

POCKET LIBRARY

THE LAND OF
BLUE MOUNTAINS

Illustrated by Maggie Downer

PARRAGON

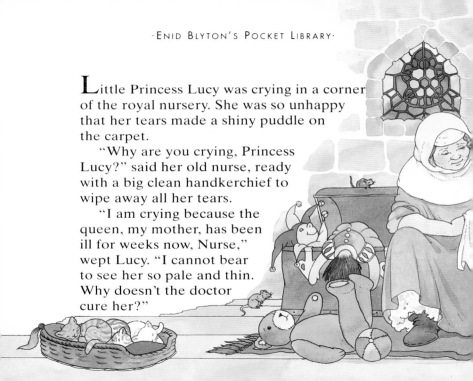

Little Princess Lucy was crying in a corner of the royal nursery. She was so unhappy that her tears made a shiny puddle on the carpet.

"Why are you crying, Princess Lucy?" said her old nurse, ready with a big clean handkerchief to wipe away all her tears.

"I am crying because the queen, my mother, has been ill for weeks now, Nurse," wept Lucy. "I cannot bear to see her so pale and thin. Why doesn't the doctor cure her?"

"Her illness cannot be cured by a doctor," said the old nurse, sadly. "A spell has been cast upon her, a spell that was cast before my very eyes!"

"Tell me what you saw," said Lucy who was now weeping faster than ever.

"I saw a little man from the Land of Blue Mountains," said the nurse. "He passed me as I lit the lamp outside your mother's bedroom. He slipped into her room and asked her for her wonderful jade necklace.

She would not give it to him so, before he left, he muttered some magic words. It was a spell I am sure! The next day she fell ill, and has never left her bed since."

"Oh, Nurse!" said Princess Lucy, in dismay. "Why should he put a spell on my mother?"

"The jade necklace came from that mysterious land," said the nurse. "And it is said that the little man who sold it to your father, the king, has always longed for it back."

"If only my father was home!" sighed Lucy. "But he is far away, exploring new lands. Who else can help my mother, Nurse?"

"No one," said the nurse. "None would dare to go to the Blue Mountains save your father."

"Where is the Land of Blue Mountains?" asked Lucy. "Tell me."

"Come with me, and I will show you," said the nurse. So Lucy followed her up hundreds of stairs until she reached the highest room in the palace. It was a little round room with one tiny round window set in the western wall.

"Look through that window," said the nurse. "It is the only window in the palace that looks upon that strange land."

Lucy saw a glorious sight. Far away rose peak upon peak of deep-blue mountains, their summits tipped with gold in the setting sun. White clouds floated round the blue mountainsides, and the valleys between were dark purple.

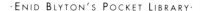

It was so strange and wonderful that Lucy longed to go there. She looked for a long time until her nurse grew tired of waiting, and told her it was time for bed.

"If I went there I might find the little man who put the spell on my mother," she thought as she climbed into bed but when she asked how to get there, her nurse said,

"Nobody knows but your father. It is a cold, stony land, and the people there have hearts as cold and stony as their mountains. Now go to sleep, Lucy, and forget all you have seen."

But in her dreams Lucy dreamt that she
was following a little humpbacked man
up a blue mountainside, calling to him
to stop. She dreamed that she came
to a well, full of gleaming,
golden water. And last of
all she dreamed that her
mother was well again.

When she woke up, the dawn was just creeping in from the eastern sky. Lucy put on her bedroom slippers and ran up to the highest room in the palace. Once more she peeped through the round window and saw the gleaming blue mountains.

But how strange! They seemed much nearer than the night before, and a broad road ran to them from the edge of the palace gardens.

In a trice Lucy had made up her mind. She would go to the Blue Mountains herself. Quickly she ran to her room and dressed. Then she went downstairs and opened the garden gate. There lay the road, gleaming like gold in the morning sun. She stepped out on to it, and as she did so, she heard a bark behind her.

It was Saxon, her dog. He had heard her footsteps and had come to join her. Lucy was so pleased to see him.

"Oh, Saxon," she said. "Will you come with me to the Land of Blue Mountains?"

Saxon licked her hand, and then knelt down beside her. He wanted her to climb on to his broad back, for he often gave the little Princess a ride.

"Oh, that is a splendid idea!" cried
Lucy. "Now we shall soon be there!"
So off they went down the
gleaming golden road, with the tall
blue mountains shining far away
in front of them, and the palace
slowly growing smaller and
smaller behind them.

After some time they came to a clear stream at the roadside, and they both drank from it. Then suddenly the dog gave a loud bark and pointed with his paw to the road behind them.

Lucy looked – and what a strange sight she saw. The road was disappearing!

"Oh, the road is going!" she cried to Saxon. "Quick! We must reach the Land of Blue Mountains before the road is quite gone!"

Off they raced, while behind them the road gradually disappeared as if someone were rolling it up. Great rocks and thick woods sprang up where the road had been. Faster and faster galloped the panting dog, and nearer and nearer came the mountains.

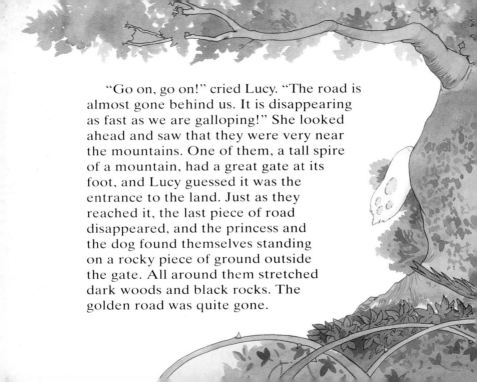

"Go on, go on!" cried Lucy. "The road is almost gone behind us. It is disappearing as fast as we are galloping!" She looked ahead and saw that they were very near the mountains. One of them, a tall spire of a mountain, had a great gate at its foot, and Lucy guessed it was the entrance to the land. Just as they reached it, the last piece of road disappeared, and the princess and the dog found themselves standing on a rocky piece of ground outside the gate. All around them stretched dark woods and black rocks. The golden road was quite gone.

The gate swung open and they passed through together. Blue mountains towered up on every side. Their sides were bare and stony, and as blue as forget-me-nots. The little streams that fell down the sides were blue too, and the only plants that grew there were great bright blue things as large as saucers.

"What a strange country!" whispered Lucy and Saxon licked her hand gently to stop her from feeling afraid.

They chose one of the paths that led between the mountains and followed it. Lucy was surprised to see no one about – but at last she spied two little figures, and she called to them. They stopped and looked at her in astonishment.

As she drew near she saw that they were dressed in blue wool, and had woollen caps on their heads. Their eyes were cold and blue, and Lucy did not like them.

"What are you doing here?" the little folk demanded. "Aren't you cold without a coat?"

"Not at all!" said Lucy, in surprise. "The sun is very warm. You must be hot in all those clothes."

"Only those with warm hearts can keep warm here," said one of the little men. "We folk of the Blue Mountains are cold, even on the hottest day. Why did you come here?"

"I came to find the little man who put a spell on my mother," said Lucy. "He once sold a jade necklace to my father, the king."

"That must be Blizzard, who lives at the top of this path," said the little folk. "But be careful of him. He is the coldest one of all."

Lucy said goodbye and took the narrow path they pointed out to her which led up the steep mountainside.

"I am so hot I don't know what to do," said Lucy after a while. "However can these people here be

cold when they have all these
mountains to climb!"

Just then a little humpbacked
man came toiling up another
path nearby. Lucy called to
him, but his sheepskin cap
was pulled so firmly
over his ears that he
did not hear her.

"Perhaps that is
Blizzard," she said
to Saxon. "Come
on. We'll
follow him."

So on they went following the little blue man up the great blue mountainside. At last he went inside a small cottage set into the hillside. Lucy and Saxon followed, and knocked loudly.

Blizzard came to the door in surprise. Not many visitors came to his cottage.

"What do you want?" he asked.

"I am Princess Lucy and I have come to ask you to lift the spell from my mother," said Lucy. "You have made her ill, and I want her well again."

Blizzard's eyes were like two shining sapphires.

"You have come to this cold, stony country," he said, "where we all shiver and freeze, and yet you have no coat and no hat. Let me feel your hand. Why, it is warm as fire!"

"And yours is as cold as ice," said Princess Lucy with a shiver.

"It is cold as my heart," said Blizzard mournfully. "All people with cold hearts are sent to live here, and we never feel warm. If only I had a warm heart like yours! How happy I should be!"

"Yes and you would be kind too," said Lucy. "It was cruel of you to put a spell on my poor mother. Tell me how to undo it."

"Why should I?" said Blizzard, his little cold eyes gleaming like ice. "You have nothing to give me in exchange."

Lucy began to cry. Her tears fell down her cheeks, and Blizzard touched them in wonder.

"Why, even your tears are warm," he said.

"I would give anything to have a heart as warm as yours!"

"Then take that horrid spell off my mother and I will give you my warm heart and take your cold one!" said the little princess, bravely.

Blizzard could not believe his ears at first, but as soon as he knew that Lucy meant what she said he took her by the hand and hurried her down the mountainside.

"We will go to the well of golden water," he said. "A bottle of that will cure your mother. Then we will go the Ice Maiden who lives at the top of the highest mountain and she will change our hearts for us. Oh, I shall be so happy when I get your warm heart for my own!"

Lucy hurried after him. On and on they went,
until they came at last to the foot of a towering
blue mountain, the highest of all, and at the very
top was a shimmering palace of blue ice. They
started up the winding path that led to the top
and had not been climbing long before they came
to a well, the same one that Lucy had seen in her
dream. She looked down and saw golden water at
the bottom. There was no bucket to send down,
and Lucy wondered how they were to get the
magic water. But the little man soon showed her.

He tied a rope round himself, knotted one end
to a post of the well, and then let himself down to
the water. He filled a bottle, and then, with Lucy's
help, pulled himself up again. Where his clothes

had touched the water he shone like the sunset.
He gave the bottle to Lucy, who slipped it into
her pocket.

Lucy felt a tug at her dress, and saw Saxon looking at her. He wanted her to climb on his back and run away without giving her warm heart to the little blue man. But she would not.

"No, Saxon," she whispered in his ear. "A princess cannot break her promise."

On they went to the shimmering blue palace and passed through a gate of blue sapphire so beautiful that it hurt Lucy's eyes to look at it. Then into a great hall they went, and the little princess saw a giantess sitting on a throne of silver.

"What do you want?" asked the Ice Maiden, and her voice sounded like ice cracking on a pond.

"This princess is going to give me her warm heart in exchange for my cold one," said Blizzard.

"Will you make the magic that will change our hearts?"

"Why do you want a warm heart?" asked the Ice Maiden. "Warm hearts are a nuisance. They make their owners do kind and unselfish deeds. It is much nicer to be cold and selfish."

"But her tears are warm!" cried Blizzard. "It must be wonderful to have warm tears and a warm heart to match!"

The giantess laughed, and it was like a shower of hail falling on a glass roof.

"If you wish it, I will change your hearts," she said. "You must hold hands and walk together to the gateway of our land. Kiss her twice when you get there, and look deep into her eyes. Then you will have her heart and she will have yours."

"Thank you," said Blizzard, and they left the palace, with Saxon following behind. Down the mountainside they went, holding hands, and as they went Lucy's hand became cold, and Blizzard's became warm.

For a long time they walked, until at last they reached the gate through which the princess and her dog had passed that very morning. It was dusk now, and the moon was rising. For a minute it went behind a dark cloud. Blizzard let go of Lucy's hand, and waited for the moon to come out again. But before it did so, he felt two kisses, and found himself looking into two eyes, while two hands rested on his shoulders.

Suddenly there came a pain in his heart and it became warm. Blizzard felt so glad that the tears poured down his cheeks and he could not see.

"My heart is warm, my heart is warm!" he cried. "I shall never be cold again! I am happy, happy, happy!"

He slipped through the gates and ran back to the Land of Blue Mountains, leaving Lucy standing alone very much astonished.

"But how can your heart be warm?" she called. "You didn't kiss me, nor look into my eyes! My heart is not cold. It is as warm as ever."

But there was no answer. Blizzard had gone.

Then Lucy felt a wet nose against her arm, and guessed what had happened. Saxon had pretended to be her, when the moon had gone behind that dark cloud! He had stood up in front of Blizzard with his paws on the little man's shoulders, and had licked him twice!

"Oh, dear, kind Saxon, you have given up your own warm heart in place of mine!" cried Lucy, hugging him. "I think you are the most wonderful dog in the world! But what has happened to Blizzard's cold heart? Have *you* got it?"

Saxon mournfully nodded his head. Then, very sadly he trotted down the road beside the princess. His heart was heavy and cold, and he felt strange and unhappy. But he also felt glad because he had saved Lucy's warm heart for her, and she had the bottle of golden water safe.

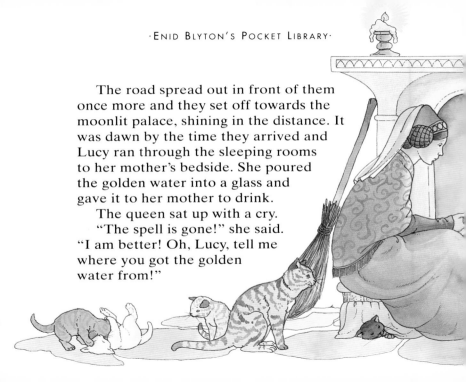

The road spread out in front of them once more and they set off towards the moonlit palace, shining in the distance. It was dawn by the time they arrived and Lucy ran through the sleeping rooms to her mother's bedside. She poured the golden water into a glass and gave it to her mother to drink.

The queen sat up with a cry.

"The spell is gone!" she said. "I am better! Oh, Lucy, tell me where you got the golden water from!"

Lucy told her story, and at the end the queen cried to think of poor Saxon and his cold heart.

"See him sitting by the fire, shivering," said Lucy. "What can we do for him, Mother?"

Just then the old nurse came into the room and cried out in delight to see Lucy, and to find the queen better once more. When she heard about the poor dog, she smiled.

"Don't fret," she said. "His heart will soon be better. No dog can possess a cold heart for long. Feed him on milk mixed with your tears for him, and his heart will be as warm as ever in a few days!"

And so his heart gradually became warmer, and his bark became happier and happier, until at last his heart was as warm as ever. The Princess Lucy was so grateful that she had a fine collar made for him, and from it she hung a tiny golden heart. He will show it to you if ever you see him!